BRISTOL SCHOOL LIBRARY
SCHOOL DISTRICT OF WEBSTER GROVES

MW01393439

DATE DUE

AP 09 '98			
MY 04 '98			
SE 15 '98			
FE 26 '99			
OCT 27			
OCT 12			
JAN 06			
OC 06 '04			
AP 07			
JAN 26			

Demco, Inc. 38-293

DEMCO

OCEANS

OCEANS

DON P. ROTHAUS
THE CHILD'S WORLD©, INC.

PHOTO CREDITS

TOM STACK & ASSOCIATES / TScott Blackman: front cover *(Otter Rock, Oregon)*, 24
TOM STACK & ASSOCIATES / Doug Sokell: 2 *(Cape Kiwanda, Oregon)*
TOM STACK & ASSOCIATES / ESA / Tsado: 6
TOM STACK & ASSOCIATES / Mt. High Maps / Digital Wisdom / Tsado: 9,19
TOM STACK & ASSOCIATES / David B. Gleetham: 10
TOM STACK & ASSOCIATES / NOAA: 13,16
TOM STACK & ASSOCIATES / Greg Vaughn: 15
TOM STACK & ASSOCIATES / EInga Spence: 20
TOM STACK & ASSOCIATES / Mike Bacon: 23
DON P. ROTHAUS: 26
TOM STACK & ASSOCIATES / Ed Robinson: 29
TOM STACK & ASSOCIATES / Jim Nilsen: 30

PHOTO RESEARCH
Jim Rothaus / James R. Rothaus & Associates

PHOTO EDITOR
Robert A. Honey / Seattle

Text Copyright © 1997 by the Child's World ©, Inc.
All rights reserved. No part of this book may be reproduced
or utilized in any form or by any means without written
permission from the publisher.

Printed in the United States of America.

Library of Congress Cataloging-in-Publication Data

Rothaus, Don.
Oceans / Don P. Rothaus.
p. cm.
Includes index.
 Summary: Describes various characteristics of the world's oceans, including
orgins, the composition of seawater, currents, and the effect of the moon on tides.
ISBN 1-56766-286-2 (hardcover : library bound)
1. Ocean—Juvenile literature. [1. Ocean.] I. Title.
GC21.5.R68 1996
551.46—dc20   96-11468
                    CIP
                    AC

TABLE OF CONTENTS

The Big Blue Marble 7

How Large are the Oceans 8

In the Beginning 11

Three Great Oceans 12

Standing at the Edge 14

The Giant Soup Bowl 17

What are Midocean Ridges? 18

What is Seawater? 21

What are Currents? 22

The Moon's Pull 25

What Lives in the Oceans? 27

Exploring Our Oceans 28

The Ocean Resources 31

Glossary and Index 32

THE BIG BLUE MARBLE

As the space shuttle *Discovery* orbits the Earth, an astronaut pauses from her task. She takes a moment to gaze out through the window toward the beautiful blue and white planet below. One of the first astronauts to view the Earth from space said that it looked like a big blue marble. Its blue color is a sure sign that the planet Earth is a world of water.

⇐ **White clouds dot the Atlantic Ocean *(left)* and parts of Africa *(right)*.**

HOW LARGE ARE THE OCEANS?

Because we live most of our life on the land, we sometimes forget how large our oceans are. In fact, three-quarters of the Earth's surface is covered by water. Most of this water is in our oceans, which cover about 140 million square miles of the Earth's surface. Of all the planets in our solar system, only Earth has oceans. The Earth also has bodies of water called *seas*. A sea is just like an ocean, but smaller and mostly surrounded by land.

The Pacific Ocean is left, and the Atlantic Ocean is right of the Americas. ⇒

IN THE BEGINNING

The outer surface of the Earth is covered with a thin, rocky *crust* like the shell of an egg. Below that is a layer of hot melted rock called the *mantle*. When these layers were forming billions of years ago, water was trapped beneath the cooling crust. Melted rock often broke through the new crust, releasing the water in huge clouds of hot steam. When the clouds cooled, the water fell back to Earth and formed the oceans.

⇐ **Hot lava turns water to steam on Fernandina Island in the Galapagos Islands.**

THREE GREAT OCEANS

There are three major oceans on earth. The *Pacific Ocean* is the largest. It is located off the western shore of North and South America. The *Atlantic Ocean* lies off the eastern shore of North and South America. The *Indian Ocean* lies just below India and east of Africa. These three great oceans join together around the continent of Antarctica to form what some people call the *Antarctic Ocean*. Can you find these oceans on a map?

The sea floor of the Pacific, Atlantic and Indian Oceans is shown in dark blue. ⇒

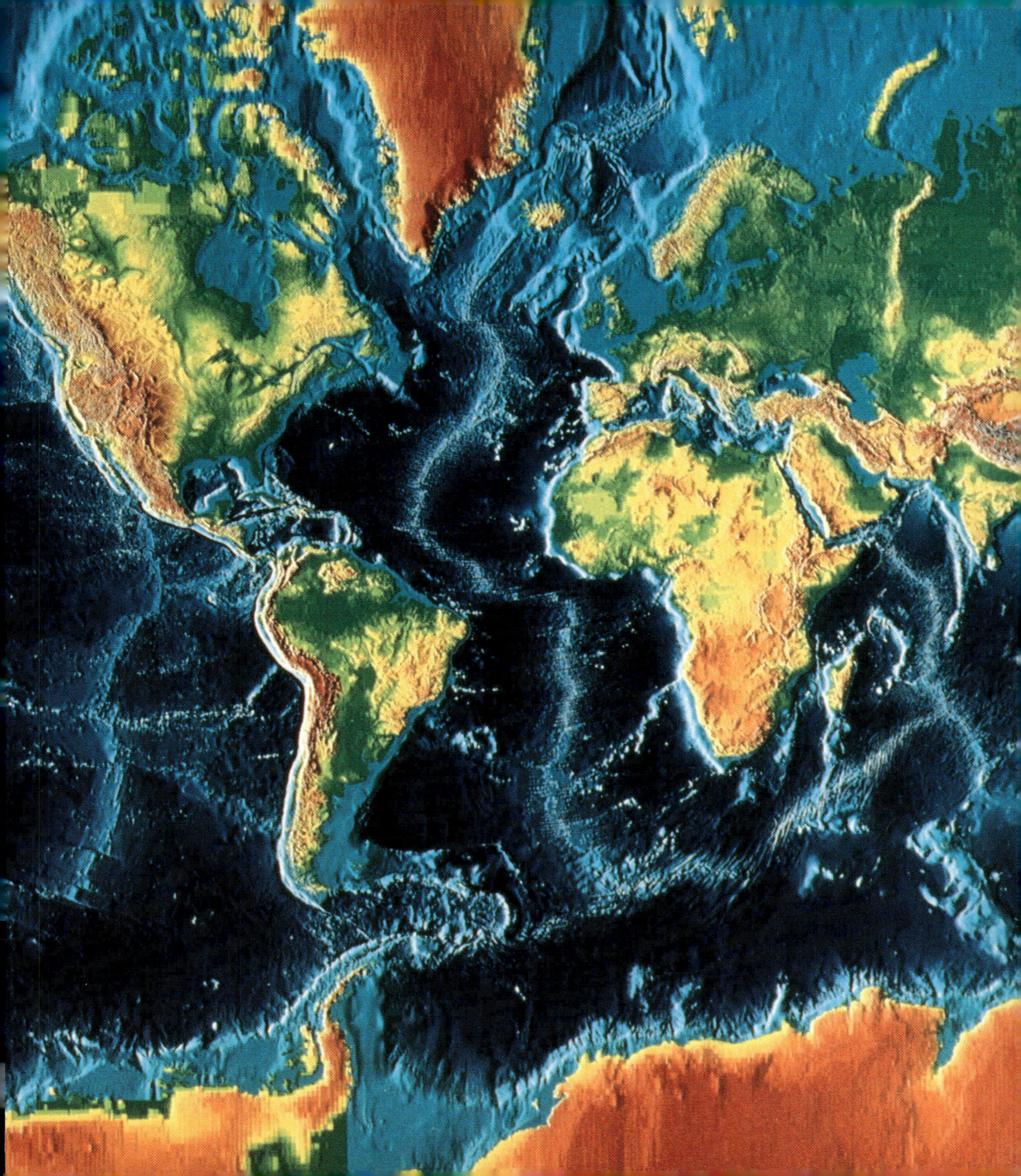

STANDING AT THE EDGE

Have you ever walked along an ocean beach? Beach sand often has many small pieces of shell and coral mixed in with the grains of sand. Beaches are constantly moving and changing as storms and waves cut and pull the sand. A beach in winter will often be very steep as a result of harsh winter storms. The same beach in summer may be flat and wide because of mild weather conditions. New sand replaces the sand that is moved by storms and waves. The new sand is eroded land that has been carried by rivers and streams to the oceans.

The beach sand on Haena Beach in Kauai, Hawaii has been ground smooth. ⇒

THE GIANT SOUP BOWL

All of the oceans of the world look similar beneath the waves. If you could see them from the side, they would look like giant soup bowls. Near the shore, the bottom slopes gently, like the rim of the bowl. At the edge of this rim, the water is about 660 feet deep. Then the bottom drops off sharply, like the steep sides of the bowl, to a depth of 12,000 feet! Beyond this steep drop-off, the slope becomes gentle once more. About 360 miles farther out to sea, the slope flattens out to form the level ocean floor.

⇐ **Light blue areas show the bowl rims, and darker blue the bottom of the bowls.**

WHAT ARE MIDOCEAN RIDGES?

Near the center of the oceans, there are huge underwater mountain ranges. These underwater mountain ranges are known as *midocean ridges*. Some midocean ridges are taller than the highest mountains on land. The mountain peaks reach toward the water's surface. Some of these mountains break the surface forming islands.

The tiny islands of Iceland are at the top of the Atlantic midocean ridge. ⇒

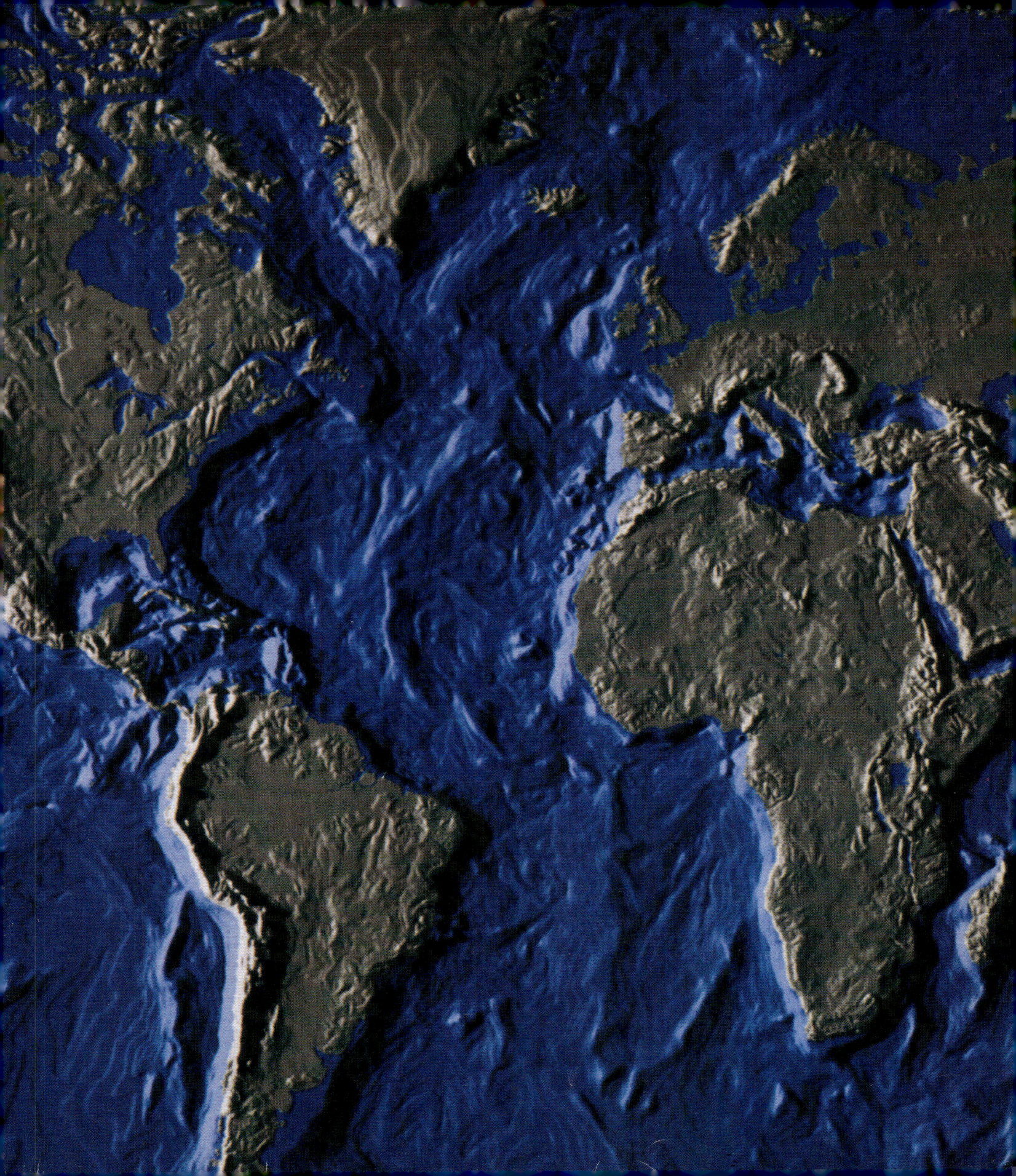

WHAT IS SEAWATER?

The water in our oceans is much different than the freshwater we drink from the faucet. Seawater is salty. Over millions of years, as rivers, streams and rain runoff eroded the land, minerals were mixed into the ocean water. The majority of the minerals dissolved in seawater are sodium and chloride—like the white salt in your kitchen cupboard.

⇐ **Small streams are still adding their share of salt to the oceans.**

WHAT ARE CURRENTS?

Wind that blows over the ocean causes the water to move in a circular pattern. These water movements are called *ocean currents*. There are many different kinds of currents. One type is called *upwelling*. These currents are caused by winds that blow offshore. Water on the ocean surface is forced away from the coast. Cold, nutrient rich water rises from the deep ocean to replace the surface water. Areas of upwelling have a huge variety of marine animals because the water is full of food and other substances useful for life and growth.

Ocean currents make it possible for large amounts of sea life. ⇒

THE MOON'S PULL

As the moon rotates around the Earth, it tugs at the ocean surface causing the water level to rise. This is called a *high tide*. After the moon passes, the water level falls causing a *low tide*. Two high and two low tides occur every twenty-five hours. The effect of tides can only be seen near land. In some places the waterline rises as much as fifty feet during a tide cycle.

Tides can cause some of the fastest currents. At narrow entrances to seas and bays the water can move at speeds of ten to twenty miles per hour during a change of tides.

⇐ **The beginning of a high tide is seen on an Oregon State beach.**

WHAT LIVES IN THE OCEANS?

A wide variety of plants and animals live in the oceans. Whales, dolphins, seals and sealions are *marine mammals* that live in the oceans. They dive to find food in the underwater world and return to the water's surface to breathe air. Colorful fish, shrimp, jellyfish, sea stars and other marine creatures spend their entire life in the oceans. They breathe by removing oxygen from the water using *gills*. Large *kelp forests* can also be found beneath the waves. Kelp is a large algae that attaches to rocks. It can grow up to 100 feet in a single season. Many marine animals live within these kelp forests.

⇐ **Ocean life varies a lot, a clown fish doesn't get stung by the sea anenome.**

EXPLORING OUR OCEANS

The oceans have many mysteries waiting to be discovered. This duty lies in the hands of the scientists who study oceans. *Oceanographers* study the physical nature of the oceans. They map the ocean floor, explore deep water trenches, and study the movement of the currents. *Marine biologists* study the plants and animals of the oceans. They look at where these plants and animals live, how they eat, how fast they grow, how they reproduce and how they interact with one another. These scientists use submarines, underwater cameras, high-tech research ships, diving gear and many other tools to try and answer the mysteries of our oceans.

A marine biologist studies soft coral off the island of Fiji. ⇒

THE OCEAN RESOURCES

We must wisely use our ocean resources. We already harvest large amounts of fish and shellfish from our oceans. As the world's population grows, we may need to use the ocean for other purposes. Soon we may learn how to mine the precious metals in our oceans. As our need for energy increases, it may be necessary to increase offshore oil exploration. With all of these additional demands, our oceans must be watched closely so that the delicate balance of our underwater world can be maintained.

⇐ **Nature can be kept in balance by catching only as many fish as we need.**

INDEX

beach, 14

crust, 11

currents, 22, 25

gills, 27

high tide, 25

kelp forest, 27

low tide, 25

mantle, 11

marine biologist, 27

marine mammals, 27

midocean ridges, 18

oceanographer, 28

seas, 8

seawater, 21

upwelling, 22

GLOSSARY

crust (KRUST)
The surface of the earth. the outer solid rock layer that rests on a layer of melted rock known as the mantle.

gills (GILS)
An organ found in fish and other marine animals that removes oxygen from the seawater. This organ allows these animals to breathe underwater.

high and low tide (HI and LO TIDE)
The rise and fall of the surface level of the oceans caused by the pull of the moon. The change in surface level may be as much as fifty feet long some shorelines.

kelp forest (KELP FOR-est)
A large brown algae that attaches to rocky bottoms and grows up to the surface. This algae grows close to one another forming underwater forests.

marine biologist (muh-REEN bi-AHL-oh-jist)
A scientist who studies marine life in our oceans.

mantle (MAN-tul)
The layer of melted rock between the crust of the earth and the core.

marine mammals (muh-REEN MAM-muls)
Marine animals that have fur or hair, are warm blooded, and must return to the surface to breathe air. Examples are seals and whales.

midocean ridges (MID-OH-shun RIJ-es)
An underwater mountain range that is found in the middle of the oceans.

ocean current (OH-shun KUR-ent)
The circular movement of surface waters of the oceans. These currents are caused by winds.

oceanographer (OH-shun-AHG-rah-far)
A scientist that studies the physical state of the oceans and the ocean floor.

upwelling (UP-WELL-ing)
A current that flows up a steeply slopping bottom caused by a wind that blows offshore. These currents bring cold, nutrient rich waters up to the surface.

seas (SEES)
A body of water similar to an ocean but smaller and usually enclosed by land.